TI

Hairy Maclary's SHOWBUSINESS

Lynley Dodd

Spindlewood

In Riverside Hall
on Cabbage Tree Row,
the Cat Club were having
their Annual Show.

There were fat cats
and thin cats,
tabbies and greys,
kick-up-a-din cats
with boisterous ways.
Cooped up in cages,
they practised their wails
while their owners fussed over
their teeth
and their
tails.

Out in the street,
tied to a tree,
Hairy Maclary
was trying to see.
He struggled and squirmed,
he unravelled the knot
and dragging his lead,
he was off
at the
trot.

He bounced up the steps,
he pounced through the door,
he pricked up his ears
and he pranced round the floor;
flapping and flustering,
bothering,
blustering,
leaving behind him
a hiss
and a
roar.

'STOP!'
cried the President,
'COLLAR HIM, QUICK!'
But Hairy Maclary
was slippery slick.

He slid under tables,

he jumped over chairs,

he skittered through legs

and he sped down the stairs.

In and out doorways,
through banners and flags,

tangling together
belongings and bags.

Along came Miss Plum
with a big silver cup.
'GOT HIM!' she said
as she snaffled him up.

Preening and purring,
the prizewinners sat
with their rosettes and cups
on the prizewinners' mat...

and WHO
won the prize
for the SCRUFFIEST CAT?

Hairy Maclary
from Donaldson's Dairy.

Other Lynley Dodd books

MY CAT LIKES TO HIDE IN BOXES (with Eve Sutton)
THE NICKLE NACKLE TREE
TITIMUS TRIM
THE APPLE TREE
THE SMALLEST TURTLE
HAIRY MACLARY FROM DONALDSON'S DAIRY
HAIRY MACLARY'S BONE
HAIRY MACLARY SCATTERCAT
WAKE UP, BEAR
HAIRY MACLARY'S CATERWAUL CAPER
A DRAGON IN A WAGON
SLINKY MALINKI
FIND ME A TIGER

British Library Cataloguing in Publication Data
Dodd, Lynley
    Hairy Maclary's Showbusiness
    1. Title
    823[J]

Published in 1991 by Spindlewood
70 Lynhurst Avenue, Barnstaple, Devon EX31 2HY.

First published in 1991 by
Mallinson Rendel Publishers Ltd.
Wellington, New Zealand.

Reprinted 1992, 1994

ISBN 0-907349-51-X

Typeset by Joe Coghlan Phototype, Wellington, New Zealand
Printed and bound by Colorcraft Ltd., Hong Kong